Yo-Yo a Go-Go

Celia Warren
Illustrated by Charlotte Hard

RIGBY

We played with our yo-yos all day at school. We all loved our yo-yos, but all our teachers **hated** yo-yos.

Mr Rust hated yo-yos.
He said, “No yo-yos!” and put up a sign.
All his children were sad.

Miss Blake hated yo-yos, too.
She said, "All yo-yos must go!"
and put up a sign.
All her children were sad.

My teacher was Mr Dodd.

He was a new teacher.

We all loved Mr Dodd.

Mr Dodd loved yo-yos, too.

He said, “Let’s have yo-yos in class next week.”

“Wow! We’re lucky!” we said.

On Monday, we did yo-yo maths.

We loved yo-yo maths.

“Wow! We’re lucky!” we said.

On Tuesday, we read yo-yo books.
We all loved the yo-yo books.
"Wow! We're lucky!" we said.

On Wednesday, we wrote yo-yo stories.

Then we read our yo-yo stories.
"We're lucky!" we said.

On Thursday, we painted yo-yo pictures.
"Not yo-yos again!" we said.

On Friday, we **hated** yo-yos.

"We don't want yo-yos at school," we said.

We took our yo-yos home.

"Wow! That's lucky!" said Mr Dodd.